My name is _____

I celebrated World Book Day 2015 with this brilliant gift
from my local Bookseller and Macmillan Children's Books

For Rosie

First published 2015 by Macmillan Children's Books
an imprint of Pan Macmillan
a division of Macmillan Publishers Limited
20 New Wharf Road, London N1 9RR
Associated companies throughout the world
www.panmacmillan.com

ISBN 978-1-4472-8247-1

Copyright © Chris Riddell 2015

The right of Chris Riddell to be identified as the author and illustrator of this work has been
asserted by him in accordance with the Copyright, Designs and Patents Act 1988.

1 3 5 7 9 8 6 4 2

A CIP catalogue record for this book is available from the British Library.

Printed and bound by CPI Group (UK) Ltd, Croydon CR0 4YY

Goth Girl

and the Pirate Queen

CHRIS RIDDELL

MACMILLAN
CHILDREN'S BOOKS

THIS BOOK CONTAINS FOOTNOTES
WRITTEN BY A LAMB CALLED CHARLES,
WHO LOVES THE PLAYS OF SHAKESPEARE

Chapter One

Ada Goth stared at the three extremely plump Dalmatian dogs opposite her. They were sitting in a row, their pink tongues lolling out of their mouths and their fat tails drumming on the carriage seat as they wagged. A terrible smell wafted through the air and Ada wasn't sure which of the Duchess of Devon's Dalmatians was responsible – Lottie, Dottie or Spottie. Perhaps it was all three of them.

Beside Ada, Lady George* snored loudly, her grey powdered wig askew. One of her moleskin eyebrows had come unglued and had slithered down her pink powdered cheek like an escaping caterpillar. Ada opened the carriage window and took in a lungful of air. They had reached the top of a hill and in the distance Ada

Lamb's Foot notes
* Lady George is a close friend of Ada's father, Lord Goth, and often takes part in his annual metaphorical bicycle race. You can read all about it in *Goth Girl and the Ghost of a Mouse*. There's a ghost in Shakespeare's *Hamlet* too.

saw the sea for the very first time.

It was broad and blue with white waves flecking its surface like breadcrumbs on a tablecloth and when Ada breathed in she could taste the salt in the air.

'Are we there yet?' asked Lady George, picking up the eyebrow that had landed in her lap and pressing it back into place on her forehead.

'Almost,' said Ada. 'This is so exciting!'

Ada was the only daughter of Lord Goth of Ghastly-Gorm Hall, a huge house in the country, and this was her first trip to the seaside. Lady George had received an invitation from the Prince Regent himself to attend the World Frock Day Ball at his new palace in the fashionable seaside resort of Brighton.

The Prince Regent

requests the pleasure of the company
of
Lady George and Companion
at
The World Frock Day Ball
(where a prize will be awarded for the most fashionable frock)
at
THE BRIGHTON PAVILION
Dress: Extremely Smart

'You must let me take little Ada with me, Goth,' Lady George had told Ada's father. 'The salty seawater will do her good. I'll see to it that she drinks two cups a day!'

Ada wasn't too sure about the cups of salty seawater, but she liked the sound of the World Frock Day Ball.

'Are the Prince Regent's trousers really as big as they say they are?' Ada had asked.

'You can see for yourself,' Lord Goth had said with a smile. Reaching into his velvet

waistcoat, her
father had taken
out a neatly
folded twenty-
guinea banknote
and handed it to Ada.

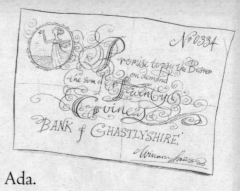

'Use this to have a fashionable frock made
for yourself,' he'd said. 'Spend it wisely!'

'Ada had thanked her father and given
him a great big hug. As a general rule Lord
Goth wasn't the sort to give hugs, great big or
otherwise. A slight nod of the head or a stiff
bow was more his style and, on extremely
rare occasions, a firm handshake. But when it
came to his only daughter, Lord Goth didn't
mind one bit. He hugged Ada back.

'You're growing up so fast,' he had whispered.
'Your mother would have been so very proud.'

Now, after two days of rattling over
bumpy highways and even bumpier byways in
Lady George's Dartmoor landau, they were
almost there.

HAMILTON AND BUTTON
THE FOOTMEN

LADY GEORGE'S
DARTMOOR
LANDAU

DARTMOOR
PONIES

They went down the hill on a chalky road, passed two windmills and arrived at a white gate. An old man in a battered straw top hat was leaning against it.

'Brighton or Hove?' he said as the carriage drew to a halt.

'Brighton,' said Button the footman.

'Just as well,' said the gatekeeper, opening the white gate to let them through. 'Hove hasn't been built yet. That'll be thrupence.'

'Hurry up and pay the man,' said Lady George from inside the carriage. 'Tristram will be expecting us for tea. Lots of cake for my lovely girls!'

The sound of fat tails thumping on upholstered carriage seats grew louder as the Dartmoor landau set off once more.

'Oh, and, Hamilton,' Lady George called to the second footman. 'Perhaps we can have the hood down for the rest of the way, there seems to be a rather unfortunate smell in here . . .'

CARRIAGE
WARDEN –
WURZEL CRIBBAGE

THE
WHITE GATE TOLL

The road became wider and, with the hood of the carriage down, Ada could see far more clearly. In the distance was a strange-looking building. It reminded her of one of Mrs Beat'em's cakes.

The building particularly looked like Mrs Beat'em's Turkish Sultan cake, with tall thin towers and onion dome roofs. It seemed to be unfinished, because Ada could see scaffolding against its walls and several large women in caps and overalls sitting on upturned wheelbarrows drinking tea.

MRS BEAT'EM'S SULTAN CAKE WITH ICING-SUGAR SULTANAS

D'URBERVILLE
THE DAIRY MAID BUILDERS
BY APPOINTMENT TO THE
PRINCE REGENT

'Cowgirl builders,' said Lady George as the carriage swept past them. 'Fine workmanship but notoriously slow. Number thirty-two Grand Parade, Button!'

They turned left and drove along a cobbled road, and the carriage came to a halt outside a shiny, newly painted door. As they got out of the carriage, it opened and Tristram Shandygentleman, the most fashionable man in England, stepped out.

'Lady George! Ada!' he exclaimed, his shirt cuffs flapping with excitement. 'Welcome to my humble abode.'

Chapter Two

Tristram Shandygentleman waved his teacup in the air, knocking a couple of glass fishing weights off the mantelpiece.

'Don't misunderstand me, ladies,' he said. 'This is the most fashionable address in town...'

His voice trailed away as the weights bounced across the floor, hit the wall and rolled back again.

'There really isn't room to swing a –' he glanced at Lottie, Dottie and Spottie, who were being fed chocolate eclairs by Lady George – 'C. A. T.' He spelled out the word.

Ada could see what he meant. Despite its impressive appearance, the door of number thirty-two Grand Parade, like all the others in the row, opened into a fisherman's cottage, and a small one at that.

'I would get the builders in to make some alterations,' Tristram continued, narrowly avoiding a stuffed halibut hanging from the ceiling, 'but they're busy finishing the Prince Regent's pavilion. We locals call it 'the palace on the pebbles'.

'It looks just like a big cake,' laughed Ada as she put down her teacup on the extremely small table at which they were sitting.

'Don't let the prince hear you say that!' exclaimed Tristram. 'He's got absolutely no sense of humour, you know. He overheard one remark I made about the size of his trousers and struck me off the guest list.'

Tristram smoothed down his immaculate shirt cuffs sadly. 'He's awfully proud of that palace of his,' he continued. 'It's based on the stately pleasure-dome of Kubla Khan't – you know, the Chinese emperor who couldn't say no. Now, do tell me, Lady George, what are you wearing for the World Frock Day Ball?'

KUBLA KHAN'T

'A black-and-white-spotted frock that I had made for me by Fabercrombie and Itch, the intellectual west London weavers,' said Lady George, throwing the last eclair to Spottie. 'To match my girls. The skirt has been designed so that I can sneak them into the party along with me! She smiled delightedly. 'Now, Ada here has twenty guineas to spend on a frock—'

'Say no more,' interrupted Tristram. 'I know just who you should see, Miss Goth. They're two of the most fashionable dressmakers in town: Lady Vivienne Dashwood and her deadly rival, Jean-Paul Goatee. They have shops on the Not-Quite-a-Palace pier.'

'Which one should I go to?' asked Ada. Her twenty-guinea note was folded up safely in the inside pocket of her black braided tunic.

'Visit both of them,' said Tristram, catching his reflection in a shell-encrusted mirror and adjusting his neckerchief, 'then choose. You can't go wrong, they're both so fashionable!'

The next day Ada woke early. Tristram Shandygentleman's spare bedroom was extremely small, with only room for a washstand, a hammock and a nautical lantern, which Ada hit her head on when she got up. Lady George was snoring in the main bedroom, which was only a little bigger than Ada's, while Tristram Shandygentleman was fast asleep in a fold-out whaler's cot in the very small drawing room downstairs.

Ada got dressed and tiptoed down the stairs and out of the front door, making

sure to close it quietly behind her.

'Good morning, young lady,' said a
voice and, looking round, Ada saw that an
immaculately dressed gentleman in shades of
dove grey had just stepped out of the house
next door. 'And what a beautiful morning it
is!' He took a pencil from behind his ear and
jotted something down in a small black book.

BEAU
PEEPS
AND
CHARLES
THE LAMB

'Baaa!' said a small lamb standing next to him on the end of a dove-grey ribbon. 'Beau Peeps, fashion diarist and gentleman shepherd.' He introduced himself with a polite bow. 'And this is my lamb, Charles.'

'Pleased to meet you,' said Ada. 'My name's Ada Goth of Ghastly-Gorm Hall. I'm afraid I don't know Brighton very well. Could you tell me the way to the Not-Quite-a-Palace pier?'

'Certainly,' said Beau Peeps. 'Just turn left and walk along the pebble beach until you come to something that looks like a palace but isn't quite. You can't miss it.'

With that, he gave another polite bow and hurried away towards the palace on the pebbles, his pet lamb gambolling beside him.

Ada patted the pocket of her black braided tunic, turned left, and set off along the pebbly beach. Several fishermen in enormous knitted smocks and oilskin hats said, 'Good morning, miss,' as she passed, and one even offered her a tin cup of seawater. Ada said a polite 'No thank you'. The sea shimmered in the morning light and little wavelets lapped at the shore, breaking over the pebbles with soft, swishy sighs. It was beautiful, and Ada couldn't resist taking off her black slippers and stepping gingerly over the stones to paddle in the water.

The seawater was cold but the wavelets felt lovely breaking over Ada's toes. She stood and breathed in the fresh sea air.

'An early customer!' said a high-pitched, whiny voice, and Ada felt two strong hands take a grip of her shoulders and pull her backwards. Before she could resist she found herself being marched up the steps of a little wooden hut on wheels and pushed inside by a red-cheeked woman with twinkling eyes.

'I could tell by your paddling that you like the seawater but are just too timid to go in, my dear, which is why I'm here to help you!' The woman unhooked a sack with arm and head holes from the wall of the hut and thrust it at Ada.

'Here, put this sea smock on and leave your clothes on this shelf above the door — that'll keep them nice and dry for you, dear,' said the woman, folding her arms and giving Ada a steely look.

'But—' began Ada.

'No "but"s, dearie, Dowdy O'Dodds the
Warrington Dipper doesn't put up with
any "but"s, "excuse me"s or "the water's too
cold"s, oh no! Once you've stepped inside my
bathing machine you have to go in for a dip!
After all, I've got my professional reputation
to consider.'

With that, Dowdy O'Dodds turned on
her heels and left the
hut, bolting the door
behind her. In the
gloom, Ada heard
her shout, 'Giddy-
up, Patrick!' and the
bathing machine
lurched into motion.

Reluctantly Ada
took off her clothes
and folded them
neatly then slipped
the sack over
her head.

DOWDY
O'DODDS

Just then the bathing machine came to a juddering halt. The bolt slipped back, the door opened and Dowdy O'Dodds reached in and grabbed Ada by the shoulders.

'It's all right!' protested Ada. 'I can go in by myself . . .'

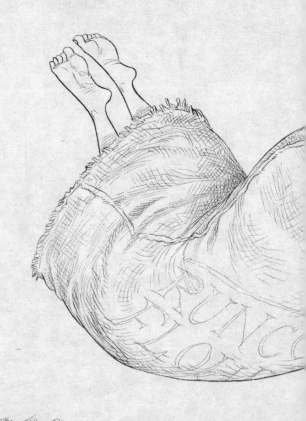

'All part of the service, dearie,' insisted
Dowdy, spinning Ada round and throwing
her through the door. Ada flew through the
air into the bright sunlight.

The next moment she landed in the
water with a great big splash and sank down
into the sea-green depths. She kicked her
legs and waved her arms and rose back
up to the surface. The sea was cold, but
Ada didn't mind. It felt wonderful. All

around her the sea shimmered in the early morning light as Ada bobbed up and down in the gently undulating waves. At home in the grounds of Ghastly-Gorm Hall, Ada went swimming in the moonlight with her governess, Lucy

Lamb's
Foot
notes

* Lucy Borgia
is a three-
hundred-year-
old vampire
who teaches
Ada umbrella
fencing, night
swimming
and poetry.
She once
met William
Shakespeare on
a midsummer
night in
Stratford-upon-
Avon. You can
read all about
her in *Goth Girl
and the Fete
Worse Than
Death*.

Borgia*, in the lake of extremely coy carp. It was fun, but nothing like bathing in the sea, with the seagulls soaring overhead and the masts of sailing ships moving slowly across the far horizon. Ada swam for a little while, enjoying the taste of the salt

on her lips and the billowing clouds, white
against the blue sky. She looked towards
the shore and was surprised to see that
the bathing machine was travelling back
towards the pebbly beach, Patrick the donkey
straining at the harness as Dowdy O'Dodds
urged him on.

'Sorry, dearie!' she called back to Ada as
she sped away in a shower of pebbles, 'urgent
business in Lytham St Annes. You can keep
the swimming smock!'

Chapter Three

A da stood on the pebbly beach and looked down at the neatly folded bundle of clothes at her feet. Without the bathing machine there was nowhere for her to change, and she wondered what urgent business had caused Dowdy O'Dodds the Warrington Dipper to hurry away like that. She put on her black slippers, picked up her clothes and was about to walk back along the beach when a squawky voice said, 'Bah humbugs! Half a pound of tuppenny bugs! Half a pound of treacle—'

'I beg your pardon?' said Ada, turning round to see a tall lady standing looking out to sea. She wore a hat with a skull and crossed umbrellas on it, a white sailor's jacket with black collar and cuffs, and carried an elegant a brass-handled sea trunk in one hand and a black parasol in the other. On her shoulder was a blue parrot.

'Oh, don't mind Roald here,' the tall lady said. She smiled, and Ada noticed that she had wooden teeth. 'He's a Norwegian blue. Used to belong to my ship's cook, Willamina Wonkers. She taught Roald to recite recipes.'

'Pour in the sugaring pan! And pop in the beetle!' squawked the parrot.

'Sounds delicious,' said Ada uncertainly. She wanted to get out of the wet swimming smock, but this stranger with a recipe-reciting parrot seemed very interesting.

'You have a ship?' she asked.

'Not any more,' said the lady, looking wistfully out to sea. 'I decided to retire after the unfortunate incident with George Washington's false teeth. Perhaps you've read about it? The story was all over the papers . . .'

'I'm afraid not,' said Ada. The lady smiled woodenly as she slipped her arm through Ada's and began to stroll with her over the pebbles.

'Well, he's not getting them back!' she said firmly. 'Not after he sank my ship. They call me the Pirate Queen, but now I'm retired I'm changing my name back to Tall Nell. It's the name the mad scientist Victoria Frankenfurt gave me.' They strolled past a fisherman brewing saltwater tea in a rusty kettle.

'No, thank you,' said Ada politely when he offered her a cup. She turned back to Tall Nell. 'My name's Ada Goth of Ghastly-Gorm Hall. Is Victoria Frankenfurt your mother?'

'In a way,' said Tall Nell. 'You see, she made me. Perhaps you've read about it? She is very talented

VICTORIA

but very competitive,' she continued, 'especially with her brother, Victor. When Victor made a monster, well, Victoria just had to make one too to prove a point. So here I am: legs of a ballerina, arms of a dairymaid and the head of a chocolatier from Mainz!'

Tall Nell let go of Ada's arm and did a balletic twirl on the pebbles. Then she paused and looked out to sea once more.

'Victor's monster and I courted for a while, but it was doomed from the start. You see, he just wanted to get away from it all, while I wanted adventure, the

VICTOR

roving life of a queen among pirates!'

'I think I've met your ex-boyfriend!' said Ada excitedly. 'He visited my house. He calls himself the Polar Explorer*!'

'That's him,' said Tall Nell, taking Ada's arm once more and resuming their stroll. 'Don't get me wrong, he's a fine figure of a monster and I wish him well, but I'm a people person, always was, always will be. My new boyfriend understands that. He's a people person too.'

'Liquorice gobstoppers!' squawked Roald on her shoulder. 'Soak your stick, roll up your gum, pinch of pepper, tot of rum!' Tall Nell smoothed the parrot's tail feathers and tickled it underneath the beak.

'With Roald's recipes, my boyfriend and I have opened a sweet shop selling fashionable confectionery here in

Lamb's
Foot
notes

* The Polar Explorer lives on an old sailing ship at the North Pole with his pet albatross, Coleridge. They don't get many visitors, which is just the way they like it. Shakespeare wrote a play called *The Winter's Tale*. If you want to know more you can read about the Polar Explorer in *Goth Girl and the Ghost of a Mouse*.

Brighton. I was just on my way there when I met you, Ada.' Tall Nell smiled and pointed with her parasol.

THE NOT-QUITE-A-
PALACE PIER

DASHWOO
LONDON · BATH
BRIGHTON

Just ahead of them was a long wooden jetty with a row of clapboard beach huts on it. Ada could see Lady Vivienne Dashwood's dress shop next to Jean-Paul Goatee's, and at the end was a beach hut with a freshly painted sign that read 'The Bolde Curiosity Shoppe: Fashionable Sweets for Fashionable People'.

A tall figure in a yellow frock coat was standing outside.

'That's my boyfriend,' said Tall Nell with a wooden-toothed smile. 'The Sherbet Pimpernel. Perhaps you've read about him. He's very dashing. Used to smuggle chocolate makers out of France during the revolution, and a brilliant confectioner, but terribly secretive.' At the sight of Ada, the Sherbet Pimpernel pulled the brim of his hat down low and went into the shop.

'And because he's so secretive I sometimes worry that nobody will discover how delicious our sweets are. Particularly this one.'

Tall Nell had

opened her sea trunk and taken out a curious-looking stripy stick which she gave to Ada.

'We call it Brighton rock,' she said. 'Take it as a memento of your visit to the seaside.'

'Thank you,' said Ada. 'It looks delicious.'

'And lasts a very long time,' said Tall Nell. She sighed. 'Not that any fashionable people have tasted it,' she said. 'Perhaps it's my pirate past or Sherbet's secretive nature, but they just turn up their noses and walk on by. We haven't had a customer in weeks, Miss Goth, and I'm at my wits' end.'

Just then the Sherbet Pimpernel poked his head out of the sweet shop and gave a secretive-sounding whistle. 'I must dash,' said Tall Nell, 'or Sherbet will over-sugar the caramel again. It really was lovely to meet you, Miss Goth.' She hurried off down the pier and disappeared inside the Bolde Curiosity Shoppe. Ada looked at the other two shops.

'Since I'm here, I might as well take a look,' she said to herself.

She walked over to Lady Vivienne Dashwood's shop, opened the door and stepped inside.

'Can I help you?' said a rather haughty-looking woman in a ginger wig, who was wearing a dress that looked as if it had been put on inside out and back to front, and enormous clumpy shoes. 'I see you're admiring my inside-out, back-to-front frock,' continued the woman. 'I'm Lady Vivienne Dashwood, radical philosopher of fashion.' She looked Ada up and down. 'You seem to be rather a radical yourself, though a little misguided,' she added, plucking at the hem of Ada's swimming smock.

'I've just been swimming,' Ada explained. 'I've got my clothes with me, if I could just use your changing room . . .'

'Oh, I don't think so,' said Lady Vivienne Dashwood sniffily. 'My changing room is strictly for radical fashion followers — to use my changing room you really have to *want* to change. Now be off with you!'

Lady Vivienne held open the door and waved Ada out before closing it firmly behind her.

Ada, a little nervously now, entered the shop next door, which had a sign that read 'Jean-Paul Goatee, Mountain Goat Couture'.

Jean-Paul Goatee clip-clopped over to greet her. 'Excellent choice, young mademoiselle,' he said, stroking his elegant tuft of a beard. His shop was full of beautifully knitted garments, all wonderfully soft to the touch.

'These are my hoof slippers,' said Jean-Paul, pointing to his boots. He took Ada by the arm and swept her through to his changing room, a small cubicle behind a cashmere curtain. 'You must put them on, they go with everything! Here, try this . . . and this . . . and – oh yes! – this . . .'

Garments of beautifully soft wool sailed over the curtain and Ada gathered them up in her arms.

'Try them on!' urged Jean-Paul, doing an impatient little clippety-clop dance on the other side of the curtain.

Ada slipped out of the swimming smock and a hand shot through the curtain and snatched it away.

JEAN-PAUL GOATEE

'Sacré bleu! This item is an outrage!' Jean-Paul exclaimed. 'I will not have it in my shop!' The door opened and closed again.

'Are you ready, mademoiselle?' came Jean-Paul's voice. 'Fashion waits for no one!'

'Nearly!' said Ada. Not only were Jean-Paul Goatee's clothes beautifully soft, they were also wonderfully easy to slip into.

'How do I look?' asked Ada, stepping through the curtain.

'Wonderful!' exclaimed Jean-Paul. 'I shall wrap them myself!' He ushered Ada back into the changing room and closed the curtain. 'Now, hurry!'

BOBBLE-HORNED ALPACA-WOOL TURBAN AND CRAVAT

STRIPED CASHMERE GOWN WITH ALPINE GOAT-WOOL TRIM

HOOF SLIPPERS

Ada changed back into her original clothes, passing the beautifully soft garments through the curtain as she did so. When she stepped out, Jean-Paul had the clothes beautifully wrapped up in a box with a ribbon.

'And how will mademoiselle be paying?' asked Jean-Paul with a beaming smile.

'I have a twenty-guinea note,' said Ada, reaching into the pocket of her black braided tunic. 'Oh dear . . .' she went on. 'I seem to have lost it.'

Jean-Paul put down the box and opened the door. He was no longer smiling.

'Au revoir,' he said.

Chapter Four

Ada walked along the pebbly beach, saying, 'No thank you,' politely every time a fisherman offered her a cup of seawater. She felt very stupid to have lost the twenty-guinea banknote her father had given her. She should have kept a closer eye on Dowdy O'Dodds the Warrington Dipper. But it was too late now and Ada had nothing to wear to the World Frock Day Ball at the palace on the pebbles. She walked back along the beach. I might not have a fashionable frock to wear, Ada thought to herself, but at least I can still enjoy the sea air. She continued along the beach towards the palace on the pebbles. As Ada approached she saw the D'Urberville builders sitting on the sacks of plaster eating bacon sandwiches and drinking tea. Beau Peeps, the fashion diarist and gentleman shepherd, was talking to them. He didn't look happy, nor did Charles the lamb, who let out bleats of agreement as Beau Peeps spoke.

'What do you mean, the ballroom won't be finished, Tess?' Beau Peeps was saying to one of the builders. He looked slightly red in the face and his dove-grey suit was lightly dusted in plaster. 'As the chief judge of World Frock Day I promised the Prince Regent personally that everything would be ready!'

'There are a lot of tradespeople involved in building a palace,' Tess explained patiently. 'Butchers, bakers, candlestick makers—'

'But what's the hold-up?' said Beau Peeps.

'Well, the butchers have been fine,' Tess replied. 'Top

quality bacon for our sandwiches. And the same with the bakers — beautifully fresh bread and tea-break biscuits.' She shook her head. 'The candlestick makers are the problem. They've let us down on the candelabras for the ballroom — nothing we can do till they get here. They said a week at best. Bacon sandwich?'

'But the ball is three days away!' protested Beau Peeps. 'What am I going to tell the Prince Regent?'

'Well,' said Tess, pouring another cup of tea and settling herself down on a comfortable plaster sack, 'I'm just a simple

TESS
OF THE
D'URBERVILLES

dairy-maid-turned-builder, not a person of refinement like yourself. But you could hold the ball in the kitchen.'

'The kitchen?!' exclaimed Beau Peeps, and Charles the lamb gave a bleat of disgust.

'I know it's not ideal,' said Tess, 'but as I've always said: you find the best people in the kitchen at parties.'

Beau Peeps looked thoughtful for a moment and then took out his small black notebook and scribbled in it.

'Interesting thought,' he said, 'but will there be enough space?'

'Biggest kitchen on the south coast,' said Tess triumphantly. 'Fit for Kubla Khan't himself!'

The other dairy-maids-turned-builders nodded their heads in agreement.

Ada walked along the pebbles, admiring the parts of the palace that weren't covered in scaffolding. The onion domes were

Lamb's Foot notes

* The Attic Club meets once a week in the attics of Ghastly-Gorm Hall, where the members discuss the interesting things they've discovered in the house and grounds. You can read about their meetings in *Goth Girl and the Fete Worse Than Death*. Thisbe is mentioned in Shakespeare's *A Midsummer Night's Dream*.

very impressive and the towers were beautifully decorated, but it still reminded Ada of one of Mrs Beat'em's cakes. Further along the beach she stopped to skim pebbles on the sea. Ada was very good at skimming. This was because she and Lucy Borgia had invented a skimming game with a circular wooden milk-pail lid from Mrs Beat'em's kitchen. They called it 'thisbe', and Ada had taught her friends in the Attic Club* to play it too.

THISBE

Ada drew back her arm and was about to skim a flat pebble across the surface of the water when it slipped out of her hand, flew through the air behind her and clunked on the hull of an upturned sailing boat that had been turned into a shop. The sign over the door read:

HORNBLOW NAVY SURPLUS STORE

A young woman with fair hair and a neatly tailored admiral's coat came out.

'I'm terribly sorry,' said Ada. 'I was skimming pebbles and one slipped out of my hand.'

'Don't worry,' said the young woman

pleasantly. 'Worse things happen at sea, and I should know as I'm an admiral's daughter.'

'I'm Ada,' said Ada. 'Is this your shop?'

'It is. I'm afraid it's all I could afford. Not as fashionable as the pier, but I'm just getting started as a dressmaker. Would you like to look inside?'

'Yes please,' said Ada.

'My name's Horatia Hornblow,' said the young woman, holding the door open for Ada.

The inside of the Hornblow Navy Surplus Store was packed with items of clothing the navy no longer needed.

There were oilskin coats hanging in rows,
deck boots lined up according to size, and
lots and lots of hats: tricornes, bicornes,
sou'westers, nor'easters and bosuns' bonnets.
In the middle of the shop was a row of

KING LUDWIG'S
BAVARIAN
BALL GOWN

THE HALF-
NELSON
SMOCK

beautiful uniforms covered in gold ribbon
and brocade which Horatia had bought from
the King of Bavaria for next to nothing when
he discovered that he didn't need a navy.

Horatia planned to alter them, she
explained, and turn them into jackets and
frocks to sell to the fashionable people
of Brighton.

MISS
AHAB'S
OILSKIN
FROCK

DAVINA
JONES'S
LOCKER
DRESS

'One day I'd like to sell them to the fashionable people of Hove,' Horatia said. 'But Hove hasn't been built yet.'

'I know,' said Ada. 'Those cowgirl builders haven't even finished the ballroom of the palace on the pebbles yet, so the World Frock Day Ball has to be held in the kitchen.'

'What a fascinating idea!' said Horatia. 'Oh, what wouldn't I give to be able to show one of my nautical frocks on World Frock Day?! The fashion diarist and gentleman shepherd Beau Peeps is one of the judges, you know.'

'Oh yes, of course,' said Ada, nodding her head sadly. 'I've been invited to the ball but I lost the twenty-guinea banknote my father gave me to buy a frock, so I don't think I'll be able to go now—'

'Twenty guineas!' exclaimed Horatia. 'Why, with twenty guineas you could have bought everything in this shop!'

She paused, then turned to Ada and smiled.

'Are you thinking what I'm thinking?' she asked.

Ada smiled the smile of someone who has discovered a really interesting fact or had a very clever thought. It was an Attic Club smile.

'I think I am,' she said.

Chapter Five

Three days later the fashionable seaside resort of Brighton was full to bursting with fashionable people eager to attend the Prince Regent's fashionable World Frock Day Ball. Anyone who was anyone in the world of fashion had been invited, and those who hadn't were thronging the pebbles behind red sash cords that the cowgirl builders had put up around the palace.

In the town the doors along Grand Parade were opening and the ball-goers, wearing heavy, tent-like capes, were making their way across the pebbles. The door to number thirty-two opened and Lady George stepped out with her three plump Dalmatians, just their paws visible beneath her large black cape. Tristram Shandygentleman walked next to her in a fashionable frock coat, and Ada walked behind. She had the hood of her cloak up and her outfit made a gentle swishing sound as she walked. A large full moon had risen over the sea and was shining down on the white onion domes of the palace.

Lady George produced their invitations at the door to the palace. The footman checked them and gave them each a number.

There was a muffled bark from beneath Lady George's cloak, which she covered up with a polite cough.

'Good luck,' the footman said gruffly.

'I'm with them,' said Tristram smoothly, slipping

in behind them before the footman could stop him.

'You old rascal,' laughed Lady George. 'My girls weren't invited either!'

They followed the stream of other guests down a wide corridor with signs on the wall saying 'WET PAINT – DO NOT TOUCH'.

And from there they went into the most enormous kitchen Ada had ever seen. Mrs Beat'em's kitchen at Ghastly-Gorm Hall was big, but it was nothing compared to this.

Four enormous plaster elephants supported the ceiling with their trunks, while the walls were lined with Chinese lacquer dressers laden with gleaming copper cooking utensils. In the centre of the kitchen four enormous ovens supported a temporary wooden walkway for the World Frock Day contestants to walk along. Three tall chairs for the judges stood opposite it, next to an upholstered throne for the Prince Regent.

'My Lords, Ladies and dedicated followers of fashion,' Beau Peeps's voice

boomed across the kitchen, 'pray stand for
the Prince Regent.'

Everybody was standing, so nobody
moved. A door next to one of the plaster
elephants opened and a man in enormous
trousers walked out elegantly.

Everybody bowed and then politely
applauded as the Prince Regent carefully
sat down on the upholstered
throne. Behind him
followed the three judges.

The guests
applauded wildly
as the judges took
their seats.

'Let the
World Frock
Day judging
begin,' boomed
Beau Peeps,
who was obviously
enjoying himself . . .

THE
PRINCE
REGENT

BEAU PEEPS, FASHION DIARIST AND GENTLEMAN SHEPHERD

EMPRESS ANNA WINTER, EDITOR OF BROGUE, THE JOURNAL OF SENSIBLE FOOT WEAR

THE JUDGES

THE SIREN SESTA, OPERA CRITIC OF HARPIES BAZAAR, THE FASHION PERIODICAL

'Contestant number one, please.'

MRS CUTHBERT
FITZCUTHBERT
WEARING
A CHOCOLATE
FEATHER GOWN
BY
MADAME
COCOA
CHANNEL

Lamb's
Foot
notes

* The Siren
Sesta stayed
at Ghastly-
Gorm Hall.
She comes
from a very
small island
near Greece.
You can read
about her in
*Goth Girl and
the Ghost
of a Mouse*.
Shakespeare
set *The
Tempest* on an
island.

'I don't approve of such sweetness,'
said Empress Anna Winter. Beau
Peeps and the Siren Sesta* exchanged
glances.

'Contestant number two!'

COUNTESS
SCHLESWIG
OF
HOLSTEIN
WEARING
A VALKYRIE
GOWN WITH
GOSSAMER
SLEEVES BY
PRINCE
KARL LARGER-FIELD

'Those slippers look too small,'
said Empress Anna Winter. The Siren
Sesta sighed.

'Contestant number three!'

LADY GEORGE THE DUCHESS OF DEVON WEARING A DALMATIAN FROCK WITH MATCHING HOUNDS BY FABERCROMBIE AND ITCH

'Far too spotty,' said Empress Anna Winter. Beau Peeps made a note in his little black book.

'Contestant number four!'

MARY
WOOLENCRAFT
WEARING
A SHEEP'S-WOOL
GOWN AND
REVOLUTIONARY
CLOGS
BY
YVES
SANS-CULOTTES

'What sensible footwear,' said Empress
Anna Winter approvingly. Beau Peeps and
the Siren Sesta shook their heads.

'Contestant number five!'

LADY RACHEL
PRETTY
WEARING A
TOADSTOOL
FROCK,
'WRECK OF
THE HESPERUS'
HAT AND
PLATFORM
SLIPPERS BY
LADY
VIVIE'NNE
DASHWOOD

'I don't approve of those slippers,' said
Empress Anna darkly. The Siren Sesta
shrugged her feathered shoulders.

'Contestant number six!'

THE
HONOURABLE
VENETIA
GOSLING
WEARING
A FAUN'S
AFTERNOON
FROCK
AND HOOF
PUMPS
BY
JEAN-PAUL
GOATEE

'I can't bear the clippety-clop!' declared
Empress Anna Winter icily. Beau Peeps
snapped shut his notebook in frustration.

'And finally, contestant number seven . . .'

MISS
ADA GOTH
OF
GHASTLY-GORM
HALL
WEARING
A MERMAID
DRESS
AND
NAUTICAL
TURBAN
BY
HORATIA
HORNBLOW

'I love that tail!' exclaimed the Siren Sesta.

'Beautifully tailored,' added Beau Peeps.

'Love those deck slippers!' trilled Empress
Anna Winter.

'What is that delicious-looking thing she's

75

holding?' asked the Prince Regent.

'I think we have a clear winner!' boomed Beau Peeps as the other judges nodded in agreement. 'The mermaid dress by Horatia Hornblow – worn so elegantly by Miss Goth!'

The ball-goers broke into wild applause, the dedicated followers of fashion noting down Horatia's name in little black books, and the fashionable ladies jotting it on the back of their fans.

Ada gathered up her fishtail and carefully descended the steps from the walkway. She approached the Prince Regent's upholstered throne and gave a curtsy, her mermaid tail swishing as she did so.

The Prince Regent reached into his waistcoat. Taking out a rolled tape measure, he unfurled it and placed it around Ada's neck.

'Please present the golden tape measure of fashionability to your dressmaker, Miss Goth,' he said.

'I'd be honoured to.' Ada smiled and
shivered with pride. She held out the stick
of rock. 'And please accept this seaside
confectionery with the compliments of Tall
Nell of the Bolde Curiosity Shoppe.' She
glanced over her shoulder at the ball-goers.
'You'll find her shop on the Not-Quite-a-
Palace pier – just ask for a stick of Brighton
rock. It's the very latest fashion!'

The Prince Regent nibbled the end of the stick of rock, and his face creased into a delighted smile.

'Delicious!' he declared.

Epilogue

Ada was delighted to get back home to Ghastly-Gorm Hall. She had had a wonderful time in fashionable Brighton by the seaside, but she was missing her father, her governess Lucy and her friends in the Attic Club. After all, she had been away for a whole month.

There had been picnic parties on the Downs, beach parties on the pebbles and supper parties in the enormous kitchen of the Brighton Pavilion. Horatia Hornblow's frocks were the talk of the town and she even had to import naval uniforms from Switzerland to keep up with the demand.

Meanwhile Tall Nell's Brighton rock had become so popular that she expanded the Bolde Curiosity Shoppe into the other beach huts on the Not-Quite-a-Palace pier, which had been vacated by Lady Vivienne

Dashwood and Jean-Paul Goatee when they had moved to Hove in a huff.

'I've brought you each a stick of Brighton rock,' Ada announced at the first meeting of the Attic Club since her return. She handed the rock around.

'This tastes delicious!' said Emily's brother William, turning the same stripy colours as the Brighton rock.

'We've missed you, Ada,' said her best friend, Emily Cabbage.

'There's lots to catch up on,' said Kingsley the chimney caretaker.

'I've oiled and polished your hobby-horse bicycle,' added Arthur Halford the hobby-horse groom.

'The best thing about holidays,' said Ada, 'is the feeling you get when you come back home!'

'Oh, I almost forgot,' said Emily excitedly. 'Some very interesting visitors* are coming to Ghastly-Gorm Hall . . .'

Lamb's Foot notes

* If you want to find out who these visitors are you'll have to wait for the next Goth Girl book!

BROGUE

THE JOURNAL OF SENSIBLE FOOTWEAR

SUMMER
ISSUE

BRIGHTON ROCK

COVER ENGRAVING BY SIR CHRISTOPHER RIDDLE OF THE SPHINX R.A.

Look out for . . .

Goth Girl

and the Wuthering Fright

CHRIS RIDDELL

Coming soon!

And also by

CHRIS RIDDELL

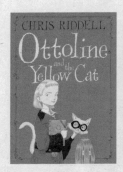

For the first time in paperback!

Turn the page to read an exclusive extract from

The Astounding Broccoli Boy

Frank Cottrell Boyce

Frank Cottrell Boyce is the award-winning author of *Millions*, *Framed*, *Cosmic* and the new Chitty Chitty Bang Bang novels. He is also a successful writer of film scripts and, along with Danny Boyle, devised the Opening Ceremony for the London 2012 Olympics. He lives in Merseyside with his family.

While the City Sleeps, an Unknown Hero Watches Over It from His Lonely Outpost on the Rooftops

Every story has a hero.

All you have to do is make sure it's you.

On my first night in Woolpit Royal Teaching Hospital, I thought my chance had come. The boy in the next bed sleepwalked. Hands straight down by his side, head held high, like a piece of spooky Playmobil he sleepwalked right up to the ward door, which is locked with a security code. I didn't want to bother the night nurse, so I followed him. He typed some numbers into the keypad. The door opened and off he went along the empty hospital corridors, through a staff canteen – where I was distracted by cheese – and out of the fire door.

I thought we'd walked on to the street.

I'd forgotten we were twelve floors up.

We were standing in the doorway of a kind of hut thing right up on the hospital roof.

Miles below, the city twinkled like a massive Christmas tree. The boy did the spooky Playmobil right to the edge of the roof. One more step and SPLAT! he would be a splodge of jam on the pavement hundreds of feet below. I thought about shouting his name, but what if he woke up, got scared and fell?

His name by the way was Tommy-Lee Komissky – though everyone called him 'Grim Komissky'. And mine is Rory Rooney. We were in the same class at school. He was the biggest and meanest. I was the smallest and weakest. I could tell you stories about the times he squashed my sandwiches, the times he threw my bag off the back of the bus, the times he threw me off the bus. But I wasn't thinking about that now. I was thinking – this is it, this is one hundred per cent my chance to be a hero.

All I have to do is save his life.

As long as he doesn't take another step, it'll be easy.

There was a flash of lightning.

He flinched.

I blinked.

There was a rumble of thunder.

He took another step.

Then Grim Komissky fell off the roof.

The Next Thing I Knew . . .

I saw him fall. I was standing in the doorway on the far side of the roof. There was nothing I could do to help him. But the next thing I knew . . .

I was standing next to him.

5

On the ground.

Between a row of wheelie bins and a skip.

I'd saved him.

I looked up at the roof twelve storeys above us.

How had we got from there to here?

How?

Well the truth is, I am astounding.

And this is the story of how I became astounding.